LIBRARIES NI
WITHDRAWN FROM STOCK

Contents

Chapter One
Gulliver House

Gulliver House. A big ugly lump of a house – and my new home.

I got out of the car and glared up at it.

'Here?' I said, giving Mum a scowling sort of look. 'You actually want me to live here?'

'Isn't it magnificent?' Mum beamed at me.

'No,' I said. 'It is NOT magnificent.'

Because it wasn't. It was even worse than the pictures Mum had showed me. Grey and gloomy. With pointy bits, and turrety bits, and skinny windows – lots and lots of them, all dark and arched and glinting.

I heaved a big sigh so Mum knew exactly how I felt.

'For the billionth time,' I said, grinding my teeth at her. 'I'm a city kid. Dragging me here is child cruelty. Where are the other houses? Where are the shops? Where are the streetlights? Where are all the other kids?'

'Finn!' screeched one of the sisters – because I've got sisters, two of them. 'You absolutely totally have to give it a chance! It's a gigantic big enormous adventure!'

I gaped at her. 'This?' I said. 'An adventure? Watching flowers grow... Listening to birdies tweeting... What am I going to do here?'

'Treasure trails,' said the other sister, eyes gleaming. 'Ghost hunts!'

Then the pair of them went skipping across the gravel and up some stone steps – built for a smallish giant – to the front door.

I trudged after them.

'There'll be spiders,' I said, giving them the glare I keep specially for the sisters. 'Great big hairy ones. Spiders grow extra big in the country. Fat legs, three inches long. And all covered in hairs like eyelashes, only seven times as thick. And they're all poisonous. Every single spider in the country is poisonous.'

'Finn,' said Mum, brandishing the key to Gulliver House like it was an Olympic gold medal. 'Stop exaggerating.'

Which is what Mum says about five hundred times a day. And I do not.

'You know what?' I warned Mum as she turned the key in the lock. 'I may be the first kid ever to actually die of boredom. And I'll probably die in a teeny tiny room up in one of those turrets, and you won't find me for months and months and when you do, I'll just be a skeleton – and then you'll be totally sorry you ruined my life.'

But Mum – instead of changing her mind and driving us straight back to the city, which is what she should have done – just ignored me.

'Our new life begins,' she beamed, pushing the big old door wide open.

★ ★ ★

Inside, I stood and gaped. How could one hallway be this big?

A vast square dark thing, stretching right up to the top of the house. With a stone staircase sweeping up one side, and a whole load of paintings on the walls. Olden days paintings – people with weird clothes, and bad hair, and staring eyes.

I shivered.

It was freezing cold in here. Full of dark doorways and shadowy corners.

I could see upstairs too, through big black railings. More dark doorways. More shadowy corners.

Mum and the sisters were already clattering around, throwing doors open, tapping walls, shrieking about hidden tunnels and secret rooms, and yelling at each other to check for loose floorboards and hidden treasure...

Which was why they didn't see it.

A slithering thing.

Something that shot across the floor. Slithered out from under a big old chest, slithered straight across the hallway and through a dark archway. So fast I just got a glimpse of it. A flash of something furry and long.

What was it? A mouse? No. Mice weren't that big. Or that shape.

Well, whatever it was, it was gone.

At least, I hoped it was.

Mum and the sisters went rushing off through a dark archway, shrieking about exploring the east wing – which I think meant one of the sticking-out end bits. The shrieking got quieter and quieter, until it was gone.

I stood in the hallway and starting counting.

There were five doors off the hallway.

Five.

I poked my head round the first door.

The room was the size of a basketball court. And depressing. Full of dark heavy furniture, the sort only old people like. With a set of grubby glass doors leading out to the garden – and a big black piano gathering dust in one corner.

The second room had the longest table in the world, and chairs round it. Twenty-two of them. Twenty-two chairs with high backs and dark arms, all draped in dust sheets, all covered in cobwebs.

The third, the fourth – more of the same. More huge rooms. More cobwebs. More dust sheets…

And it was in the fifth room that I saw the slithering thing again.

The fifth room had bookshelves, lots of them. Big heavy books rammed tightly in, floor to ceiling. And a creepy stuffed pet in a case. A glum-looking dog with long floppy ears, and a label…

WOLFGANG

Beloved companion of
Darwin Gulliver

It also had a desk with lots of drawers – and the slithering thing shot out from underneath it.

It slithered out, whipped across the room, then disappeared under a bookshelf... somehow.

I rubbed my eyes.

What was it? A snake? No. Because – just for a second – I thought it had tusky sort of things and red popping eyes.

That couldn't be right.

All the same, I felt a shiver – a teeny tiny shiver – crawl up and down my spine.

★ ★ ★

Later, up on the landing, the shiver grew bigger.

I was lugging a box of my stuff up the stairs. The stairs were long, the box was heavy, so at the top, I stopped and put the box down. Right by the landing window.

Outside, the sun was almost gone. Bulging and red, sinking slowly behind lots of spiky black trees. Sending big dark shadows like giants' fingers creeping across the landing.

Then I heard a sound. A faint faraway sound. A booming sound. Coming from somewhere out there in the twilight. Somewhere far down the garden.

And I saw something.

Something scuttling fast across the garden, almost a blur. Just a glimpse – of paws and bristles and teeth.

Then…

No. I blinked. That was wrong. I must have imagined it.

Because as it scuttled I thought I saw sparks. Sparks and tiny flames. As if, well – as if the bristling thing was breathing fire.

And even though I told myself I was wrong, that it was a trick of the light, the sun setting, flaming red and sinking down behind the trees… even though I told myself all that, still the shiver got bigger.

Just a bit.

Chapter Two
The Thing in the Wardrobe

One in six million. That's how much chance we had of moving into Gulliver House.

Because, you know why we're here?

Mum won it in a raffle.

Whoever it was who owned Gulliver House decided a raffle was the best way to sell it. So he set up a website – *winacountrypile.com* – stuck a photo of Gulliver House on it, and sold raffle tickets for a tenner each.

Six million grown-ups bought one.

Six million grown-ups – probably enough grown-ups to stretch right round the entire globe, holding hands – actually wanted to win Gulliver House…

Including Mum. Who did.

Mum also won all the horrible old furniture. And I was sitting in my bedroom, glaring at some of it right now.

It had to go. The whole lot.

The bed – which I was sitting on – was too big, too wide, too lumpy. The chest of drawers was ugly and dark and taller than me. The mirror was all scratched, and it glinted. The rocking chair had a hard bony back, and it creaked every time the wind rattled at the skinny windows. Which it did quite a lot.

Then there was the wardrobe.

Towering up in the corner like a gloomy black shadow. Huge. Big enough to walk inside, and full of fur coats.

The sisters took one look at it and – of course – grabbed hold of the doors, pulled them wide open and barged their way through all the fur coats, going, ooh, maybe we'll find a gateway to a faraway land and meet a friendly faun…

They didn't.

★ ★ ★

I started unpacking. Right now I just wanted one thing. My most precious possession.

14

My photo of Dad.

I can't remember Dad. Not one thing.

I was a toddler when it happened. When Dad went off on his motorbike one day, and had a big skid, and never came back.

Mum says he was a good dad, and he looks it. He's grinning in the photo, but scruffy – like he thinks grinning's important, but looking neat isn't.

Dad was an actor, Mum says. But he didn't get enough jobs. So he changed to being a stunt man, then he did get jobs. Dad leapt off tall buildings and through fire. He jumped off trees on to bolting horses. He wrestled with lions…

But he was going to the cake shop when he had his skid.

'I wish you were still here,' I grumbled at the photo, because I often have a chat and a grumble with Dad. 'There's not enough boys in this family.'

Then I gave his photo a quick hug, and put it on the table by the bed, so I could see him grinning at me.

I got under the duvet, and tried to find a bit of bed without lumps to lie in.

The light by my bed didn't do much. Just made a small pool of light – which left a lot of dark. Much too much dark.

Not like my old room. My tiny cosy room, where my bedside light lit up every corner. Where I could hear the sisters through the wall, and Mum clattering round the kitchen.

I felt my eyes go all round the room. Past the chest of drawers, looming… The mirror, glinting… The rocking chair, creaking… The windows, rattling… The wardrobe –

Oh no.

The wardrobe door was open. Again.

It just wouldn't shut. Not properly. It kept swinging open, just far enough open for me to see a small dark sliver of its insides.

I tried not to think about *The Hand*. That's a book I once read with a boy just like me – new house, new bedroom. A boy who woke up to see a huge scaly hand with seven bony fingers hanging out of his wardrobe.

And just as I was trying not to think about *The Hand* – and failing – I heard a small rustling, ripping sort of noise.

Coming from inside the wardrobe.

I could NOT lie there and listen to something

rustling. Not now I was thinking about *The Hand*.

I jumped out of bed, pounded right across the floorboards and flung the wardrobe doors wide open.

I pushed my way through the coats until I found it.

A chrysalis. A really big one – big as a fat sausage. Cracking right down its middle.

Brilliant!

I crouched down. This I had to watch.

Because it's like magic, what happens in a chrysalis. It's like shapeshifting. A caterpillar goes in as a wriggling wormy thing, stays in there a bit and – hey presto – when it comes out it's a butterfly.

And something was hatching right now.

I crouched closer.

This was going to be some butterfly.

I saw antlery bits first. Two waggling antler things poking out. Then a furry head – mainly bulging eyes, shining and black.

Then it crawled out.

Woah. I backed off.

It smelt bad, like rotting things. It was sludgy green and covered in slime. It was stretching out two sets of scaly wings, and flapping them, trying to dry off. Then it looked straight at me.

And it hissed.

I knew then, it was NOT a butterfly. And whatever it was – a moth, perhaps? – it was horrible.

So I turned and hurtled out of the wardrobe so fast I shot across the room, and fell straight over the box I had been unpacking.

Which meant I tried to grab hold of something to stop myself falling, only I grabbed hold of a curtain and the whole thing – pole, curtains, everything – came tumbling down.

Then the moth thing came flapping out of the wardrobe. And it wasn't much of a flier, not yet, so it flapped around the room, dripping slime, and bumping into things, and flapping between me and the windows.

So I grabbed hold of my skateboard and started waving it around in front of me, trying to stop the moth thing flying towards me, while I tried to get a window open.

Except...

Clang.

My skateboard smashed straight into the mirror and a great jagged line split the glass, then the

whole mirror clattered off the wall and shattered into bits on the floor.

And then I did get a window open, but as the moth thing flapped through, one of its horrible slimy wings brushed across my face.

I couldn't help it. I just couldn't help it. As I slammed my window shut behind it, I let out a screech – a big piercing girly screech.

Mum heard it, and so did the sisters. They all came running.

Mum took one look at my bedroom – at the smashed mirror, the curtains in a heap, everything – and started glaring.

'It was a moth thing,' I said. 'I had to chase it out.' Which sounded feeble, even to me.

And after Mum went, I checked the window. Made sure it was tight shut. Because I didn't want to see that moth thing again.

Not ever.

Chapter Three
The Piggy Princesses

My sisters are called Lily and Mo – but I don't call them that. I call them the PPs, the Piggy Princesses.

It started the day – years ago – they said I had to be a frog in their princess game, and I said I was only playing if I could be a pig. So they sat on me, both of them. For a long time.

And you know what?

If I could swap the PPs for a pair of real-life pigs – well, I probably would.

Because Mum gave us all a choice about moving to Gulliver House. Sat us all down. Said moving to the country, leaving our friends, starting a new life, would be a big change. Said we'd vote on it. Said if it was only her who voted yes to going, we wouldn't go.

And all the PPs had to do was vote against it.

But did they?

No.

Because the PPs thought moving to Gulliver House was a brilliant idea.

But it wasn't. And I had a plan to show them it wasn't. Oh yes indeedy.

★ ★ ★

I woke early next morning – too early – because the garden was twittering and rustling and making a lot of noise.

I started my plan straight away. Got dressed, crept along the landing, stopped outside the PPs' bedrooms – and tied their door handles together.

That way they'd wake up, go to open their doors, and fail. And the more they tried, the more they rattled, the more they pulled, the tighter the knots would get…

Simple, yet effective.

Then I shot off downstairs, through the hallway, along the corridor, into the kitchen, and unbolted the back door.

My first proper look at the Gulliver House garden…

And my heart sank.

A huge great garden, sweeping all round the house. Sprawling and wild and neglected. With things – dark green things, thorny things – creeping and climbing wherever they could.

A fence all around it, caging it in. And beyond it, fields. A cold grey lake. More fields. Hills. And sky. And clouds.

That was it.

Nothing and no one around.

Mum says the garden just needs someone to love it – well, not me. Because I would never ever love this garden. NEVER.

And far down on the left, dark spiky trees. Lots and lots of them. Stretching away from the garden right into the hills. The sort of forest evil woodcutters lurk in. The sort of forest where wolves dressed as grannies wait to gobble up soppy little girls.

And, poking up between two of the trees on the edge, a chimney pot.

There was a house. An actual house.

I started running. There might be a boy there. A boy who liked things I like. A boy who'd talk about interesting things – like how many marbles can fit inside a guitar, or which would be worse, to have your fingers eaten off by a rat or a badger.

But really, I thought, as I squelched through the grass, all squishy and soggy under my trainers, I didn't care if he was a boy who liked playing the violin and reading poetry. Any boy would do. Any boy at all.

And there was a boy.

Not in the garden, but in the grassy fenced-in bit next to it. Which had a sign on it, drawn in very wobbly writing. **MY PADDOCK**. With a picture of a scary monster on it.

That's where the boy was.

A short boy. Very short. With bobbing curls, and dimples. A boy who was about four years old.

Now, I know about four-year-olds, because Karim – my best friend, who lives downstairs from me in my real home back in the city – has one.

And Karim's four-year-old is boring and annoying, and always getting in our way. Always wanting to join in. And he spends every single day dressed as a superhero and all he talks about is his imaginary superpowers. Nothing else. Except sweets.

In fact, there is only one thing in the whole world more boring and annoying than four-year-olds, and that's babies.

This four-year-old had seen me and he was running across the paddock thing. Only he wasn't quite running. He was more like... well, cantering. And he was tossing his head and growling.

He skidded over to the fence. 'I'm Oliver,' he said.

He looked straight up at me. He had a solemn face, round staring eyes, and red cheeks.

'Now you have to tell me who you are,' he said. 'Because I can't talk to strangers. Mummy says.'

'Finn,' I said, feeling glum.

'You can play my game, Finn,' said Oliver. 'But you have to do this.'

He started grunting. He tossed his head. He gnashed his teeth and stamped his foot. Then he puckered up his mouth and gave a big roaring breath out. Then he raised his arms and waggled them above his head.

I gaped. What was he doing? Was this what kids were like in the country?

'I'm being the monster with the big curly horns,' Oliver said. 'And now it's your turn.'

Then he stood and waited.

What? Well – he could carry on waiting.

'Oliver,' I said, crouching down to his height. 'Do you have a brother?'

'Yes, Finn,' said Oliver.

'Can you take me to your brother?' I said.

'No, Finn,' said Oliver.

I tried not grind my teeth, but it was hard.

'Why not?' I said. 'Is he still asleep?'

'He might be,' said Oliver. 'But I don't know. Because Mummy's still growing him. But he's hatching very soon. And his name will be Arthur Jonathan Middleditch.'

Great. A four-year-old and a baby.

Then Oliver stamped his foot again and did another roar. 'When are you playing my game?' he said, looking stern. 'Because I've been waiting an astonishingly long time.'

I was saved the bother of answering because three piercing shrills on a whistle blasted out from Oliver's garden.

'That's Mummy's signal,' said Oliver. 'It means I have to go and tell her where I am.'

He pawed the ground with his foot and tossed his head again. 'I wish I had a monster tunnel in *my* garden,' he said. Then off he cantered.

Chapter Four
Twin Club

The PPs were not happy with me tying their doors together – and nor was Mum. In fact, Mum spent almost ten minutes telling me exactly how not-happy she was.

So I spent almost ten minutes telling Mum how it was all her fault for having such a stupid hobby – which is entering competitions – in the first place. And how she should have a proper Mum-hobby, like knitting or baking. And how if she *did* have a proper Mum-hobby, I wouldn't be in Gulliver House, tying doors together.

And Mum just went *grrr* and marched off, muttering something about finding a way to make me see that Gulliver House was the perfect place for kids, even if it killed her, which it probably would.

Well, I didn't care.

My plan had got off to an excellent start, and there was more of it to come. A lot more. Which was why, five minutes later, I was creeping along the upstairs landing...

Because the thing about a big landing that sweeps round the whole upstairs of the house, above the hallway, is this.

It is the perfect place to ambush sisters.

I crouched down, and poked my water cannon — pump-action Mega Blaster, 612 series, five-litre tank, ten-metre firing range — through the railings. Then I waited.

It didn't take long.

The PPs came through the hallway — skip skip skip, chat chat chat, gasp gasp gasp — discussing the map they were planning to make of Gulliver House and its garden.

But I had other plans for them...

I put my finger on the trigger, and I fired. Half a tank each — more than enough for a decent drenching. And the PPs stood there, screeching and dripping — and also blue, because I'd mixed in some paint as a finishing touch — then they charged up the stairs straight past me, glaring and hissing.

They headed for the bathroom, like I hoped

they would. Because I knew what was about to happen.

It did.

There was a thud. The sort of thud a big bucket of flour makes, falling from above a bathroom door. Then screeches, lots of them. The sort of screeches sisters would make if a big bucket of flour landed on their heads.

★ ★ ★

Once the PPs got cleaned up and dried off, they came barging into my room.

'You will be sorry,' screeched Mo. 'Sorrier than the sorriest brother who ever lived in the whole history of TIME!'

Lily nodded, eyes glinting. 'All that,' she said. 'And more.'

'Ooh, I'm scared,' I said – but actually, I was a bit. Which was why I was wearing the knee and elbow pads I use for skateboarding.

Because the PPs may look like real girly-girls – bouncing curls, big blue eyes, frilly glittering things, and way too much pink – but they're not.

They're tough. Tough like gladiators are. And sometimes they attack. Except they do cheat fighting, hair pulling and jabbing and pinching instead of proper rolling about – and it hurts. Especially when Mo does it.

But they didn't attack. Not yet anyway.

'This is one of your plans,' hissed Mo. 'I know it is! One of your stupid, stupid plans!'

Now, that was unfair. My plans are never stupid. It's just the PPs have trouble understanding their brilliance.

And, clearly it was time to explain this particular plan. So I did.

'Did I do traps or ambushes back home?' I said. 'No. Because the flat was small. So I couldn't. But Gulliver House is big. So I can.'

I thought that would explain my plan. But for some reason the PPs didn't seem to get it. So I explained more.

'I'll be doing about twenty – say twenty-five, tops – traps and ambushes each day we are here,' I said. Then I paused and waited for the PPs' teeth to start clacking with terror. But the PPs' teeth weren't clacking at all. In fact, they were grinding.

In my head my plan had worked better than this.

'So… you tell Mum you want to change your vote,' I said, starting to feel a bit less confident.

'Then we'll go back to the flat, and I won't do traps or ambushes.'

There. Clear as clear.

A simple plan – but I had to act fast. No one had bought our flat, not yet, so we could still go back. If we hurried.

Mo got it. 'Blackmail? Threats?' she said.

'Yes,' I said.

'You idiot!' Mo said, gaping. 'You actually think that will work? That me and Lily will vote to go back? To a flat with a view of the car park? A flat that shook when lorries drove past? A flat that was so small even the mice complained about the size of the kitchen cupboards? When we could live here? Here! With nineteen rooms – including one that Mum is going to turn into our very own games room – and a garden, and a lake, and an actual maze?'

Well, when Mo put it like that my plan sounded stupid. Which it wasn't.

'The flat was cosy,' I said.

'It was teeny tiny!' Mo shrieked. 'It was squashed!'

'I liked being squashed,' I said, and I was feeling grumpy now so I didn't bother explaining any more. How it wasn't just the flat I missed. It was everything. The friends, the streets, the places, the life, everything I knew.

Lily just stood there, shaking her head and looking at me pityingly – which I didn't like. 'There is no way we are the same species,' she said.

Then she turned to Mo. 'Let's go,' she said, eyes glinting. 'We have a plan to sort out.' And they left.

★ ★ ★

Half an hour later, they came back.

'See this?' said Lily.

'And this?' said Mo.

I gaped.

The PPs were standing in my bedroom doorway looking smug, like they'd just found the answer to a tricky long division sum. They were wearing matching outfits, with matching scrunchy things pulling their curls into matching knots on their smug heads. And they were both pointing their fingers at the big badges they were wearing.

Home-made, girly-looking badges, all sparkly, with little flower decorations around the edge – and big swirly silver lettering in the middle:

'That's what we are now,' said Mo, sticking her nose in the air. 'That's what happens when you try to blackmail sisters. That's what happens when you ruin the most exciting thing that has EVER happened to us!'

'And...' said Lily, smirking right in my face. 'As long as you keep doing ambushes and traps, we'll keep doing Twin Club.'

Then they marched off along the landing and towards the stairs, and Mo started talking loudly about how they were making hot chocolate – for Twin Club members only.

Now – maybe you're thinking, so what? It's only a stupid girly club. And who wants a badge with silver swirly lettering anyway? Who cares?

Well, I did. However hard I tried not to, I did.

Because the PPs are NOT twins. They're triplets – with me.

So I had to do something about their stupid plan. And as their rooms were empty, I could.

Which was why, one hour later, Mum slapped a piece of paper down in front of me. My ransom note.

To the Piggy Princesses

I have your hairbrushes,
Also the frilly things you stick in
your hair,
Also your pink socks with the
strawberries on,
Also your books on ballet,
Also your bottles of smelly stuff,
Also your metal thing that says it
curls eyelashes,
Also your box with the nail paints in
it,
Also your secret diaries.

Destroy your Twin Club badges or you
will never see them again.

'Go and get them,' said Mum. 'Wherever you put them, go and get them. RIGHT NOW.'

Which was how I saw the moth thing again.

Chapter Five

Bunnies

I saw it from the barn. I'd just scooped up the bin bag with all the PPs' stuff in it, and I saw it through a window with a broken pane of glass.

It was near some falling-down old sheds that looked like animals might once have lived in them. It was perched on a clump of big spreading planty things with fat green leaves.

But was that really the moth thing?

I crept out of the barn door, and peered round the side. I had to make sure I was actually seeing what I thought I was seeing.

I was.

The moth thing was double the size. Big as a budgie. And horribly waggly. All of it waggled. The antler things. The spare legs. The long fat end bit.

Waggly and furry. Horribly furry. A fat furry head. A fat furry middle. A fat furry end. Sludgy green fur, with black stripes.

I always thought furry things were cute – little furry puppies, little furry bear cubs…

Well, this wasn't. It was not cute at all. It was ugly. Mean looking.

And it had teeth.

Because then it tore a great strip off the fat green leaf. Slashed at it with little razor-sharp teeth, left the edges all jagged and ripped. Then it unfolded two pairs of scaly green wings, stretched them wide – and flew off, flapping and swooping like a bat does.

That was it. I was running away. Going back to the city, where there were no moth things. I had not seen one single moth thing in the city. And nothing that doubled in size in one day.

What if there were more moth things? Maybe there were caterpillars busy shapeshifting into horrible moth things in other wardrobes in Gulliver House right now. Or in cupboards. Or under the stairs.

Maybe we'd have a plague of moth things…

No.

I was packing. I was not staying one second

longer in Gulliver House. Not with a plague of moth things about to happen. And there was nothing Mum could do that would change my mind.

Not one single thing in the whole wide world...

Except, when I charged into the kitchen, Mum and the PPs were in there. And so was a box, filled with straw. And in the box were three little snuffling, twitching, soft fluffy shapes.

Bunnies.

Whatever me and the PPs argue about, we all agree on one thing, bunnies. Every year since we were big enough to write, we all put one thing at the top of our birthday list.

Bunnies

When we were six we made a stuffed bunny from my old school socks. Lily made two floppy bunny ears. I made a stuffed sock body. Mo made a pom-pom for a tail.

We called it Alice Bunnikins Sniffler – one name each. We made it a basket to sleep in, we left it bowls of food, we gave it cuddles. We dragged it behind us on a lead to the park.

It didn't work.

'A city flat with no garden is no place for bunnies,' Mum always said. 'Bunnies need fresh air, and a hutch outdoors.'

But now, here they were.

Bunnies. One each.

And Mum was smirking right in my face. 'Gulliver House is the perfect place for bunnies,' she said.

Well, I didn't care about the smirk. I was too happy. And anyway, Mum was right.

I called my bunny Thunderpaws. He was black and fluffy, with a little pink nose, and twitching whiskers.

Me and the PPs had a truce. We did our special three-way handshake – complicated and in eleven bits – which we've done since we were five.

No more traps. No more ambushes. No more Twin Club. A new start.

Me and the PPs spent the rest of the morning trying to teach our bunnies to sit. Because we saw on TV that humans only use ten per cent of their brains. So we reckoned maybe bunnies did too. In which case, they could learn to sit. Definitely…

They couldn't.

Not Thunderpaws. Not Cho Chang. Not Tinkerbell. They were lovely. They were sweet. They were funny. But however much of their brains they were using, it wasn't enough.

So that afternoon me and the PPs made them comfy in the new hutch Mum got, and started on a map of the house and garden.

Which was when I realized something.

Gulliver House had an extra window. One more window on the outside than it did on the inside – which could only mean one thing.

A secret room.

★ ★ ★

'It has to be in here,' I said. 'It can't be anywhere else.'

Me and the PPs were in the fifth room. The study. The extra window, the one in the secret room, was between the sitting room and here.

We checked the sitting room first. We hauled everything away from the wall. There was nothing behind the furniture. Just a blank wall.

So it had to be here. Somewhere behind the wall with the floor to ceiling bookshelf, and the desk and Wolfgang, the stuffed dog in the case.

'It's the bookshelf! Mo said confidently. 'It's

40

always the bookshelf. There'll be a secret button, or a special book. Some way to open it. And the whole thing will swivel round – whoosh – and it'll be there. The secret room. And there might be skeletons and tragic family secrets. Or there might be treasure. And there'll definitely be cobwebs. And I'll find it, I'll totally find it!'

Then she started hurling books out of the shelves, still babbling.

While Mo did that, me and Lily did proper checking of the room.

We lifted Wolfgang and his case off the wall, and checked behind. We pressed things. We pulled things. We looked for hidden levers or a special key. We went through the desk looking for a hidden drawer. Anything.

It was no good. We could NOT find a way into the secret room.

But we did find something – a box full of old newspaper clippings. Going back ten, even fifteen years. The newest one on top was dated three years ago…

UFO OR GIANT BIRD?
MYSTERY SIGHTING ON MOORS

And the second…

BLACK BEAST WITH HORNS
STALKS PARK, CLAIM LOCALS

And the third…

LLAMA MISSING FROM ZOO.
LARGE PAWPRINTS ONLY CLUE

They were all like that. Every single clipping. Missing animals. Strange sightings.

Now – maybe at that point I should have thought, why? Why did someone collect all those clippings? What does it mean? And maybe I should have thought more about my own strange sightings in Gulliver House. And about Oliver and his monster tunnel. And about the moth thing, and how fast it was growing…

But I didn't.

Because I was far more interested in finding the secret room.

And pizza.

Chapter Six
Feeding Time

Gulliveroni Pizza, we called it. Mum made dough, then me and the PPs rolled it out and did toppings.

We guzzled great slices of it and started planning a new teaching method for the bunnies. And the kitchen was warm now, and felt cosier, and I was beginning to wonder if I had been a bit hasty with all the traps and ambushes – and then I saw it.

A fat furry face, two slitty nostrils, two bulging eyes. Staring in through the kitchen window, straight at me.

It stuck its head on one side, and I swear its eyes – its horrible bulging eyes – started gleaming.

It looked… well, it looked like it knew me.

I shrieked, and I dropped my slice of Gulliveroni

pizza. But by the time the PPs looked out of the window, it had flapped its wings and flown off.

And — I just couldn't help it — I told the PPs about it. How it hatched from a chrysalis the size of a sausage. How it had stripes and grew big as a budgie. How it had teeth and crunched leaves and it must have a gigantic insect brain because it had recognised me…

Big mistake.

Mo started giggling. She jumped up on her chair. 'Help!' she shrieked. 'A mouse — a purple one — the size of a puppy! And it's reading a newspaper!'

She thought that was funny. I didn't.

Lily didn't giggle. She stared at me, baffled. 'This had better not be some kind of stupid plan,' she said. And she looked fed up.

I knew why.

Today had been good, and Lily didn't want me to mess it up. Well, nor did I — and I didn't…

But the moth thing did.

★ ★ ★

I was brushing my teeth when I heard screeches. Big angry screeches blasting out of Lily's room, and out of Mo's room.

44

I had a feeling the screeching was bad news –
and I was right.

I came out of the bathroom. The PPs were
standing on the landing, both waving their pjs in
my face.

Lily was glaring and looking totally fed up.

'Idiot! Why?' screeched Mo, bright red and
gnashing her teeth. 'Why? We had fun today! Why
did you have to go and RUIN it?'

I gaped.

It was their pjs. Both pairs. They had holes in
them. Big jagged holes – like something had been
tearing great big bites out of them…

Like a moth thing, hungry because it was
growing so fast.

★ ★ ★

That night my dreams were all muddled. Full
of slithering things wearing Twin Club badges,
and fire-breathing sisters, and moth things eating
pizza.

Next morning I came out of my bedroom and
stepped straight on a sheet of paper. Which had
writing on it:

STEP ON ME IF YOU'RE AN IDIOT

And I could see – even from this far away along the landing – that the PPs had stuck big notices on their doors. One on Lily's:

TWIN CLUB MEMBERS ONLY

And one on Mo's:

FINN!!! KEEP ABSOLUTELY OUT!!! FOREVER.!!!

And in the kitchen, I found a note on the table from Mum:

GONE TO GET MILK.
BACK IN FIVE MINUTES.
FINN, DO NOT DESTROY THE KITCHEN.

I sat at the kitchen table, glaring at nothing in particular.

It was quiet down here. Just the hum of the big boiler in the cellar below, the *tick tick tick* of the grandfather clock...

And a slithering noise.

It was outside. I could see it through the side window, slithering across the driveway. Gravel must be a lot harder to slither across than floorboards, because it was slithering much slower. Which meant I got a good clear look at it...

And I had even less idea what it was.

It was about as long as a ruler, with a mousey sort of face – only with red popping eyes, big flapping ears and three pointy tusk things sticking out each side where whiskers should be.

And that was it. The rest of it was a tube. A slithering furry tube, dragging a long mousey tail behind it.

And whatever it was, maybe those red popping eyes were blind – because it was slithering straight towards a flowerpot. Any second it was going to crash straight into it.

Except it didn't.

Because it flattened itself. Completely. Went flat as a sheet of paper. Slithered straight under the flowerpot, came out the other side, and popped back into shape again.

I gaped. What was it? What species, even?

Well, it didn't really matter – because the moth thing got it.

Two jets of green foam shot out from high up a tree. They hit the slithering thing, which stopped, mid-slither.

I felt my mouth drop open. What happened? Was it dead? Stunned? Frozen to the spot? What?

Then the moth thing appeared. It came flapping down from the tree, swooped on the slithering thing, picked it up in two of its long bony legs, and flapped off.

That shiver was back now. Big time. Because the moth thing had got as big as a cat.

I had to do something.

★ ★ ★

'Mummy,' said Oliver. 'Finn wants me to show him the monster tunnel in his garden.'

Oliver's mum beamed at me. 'How kind of you,' she said. 'Oliver loves playing the monster game. He pretends your garden's full of them.'

'It's not pretend, Mummy,' said Oliver, tutting. Then we went out of his back door and down the garden.

Now, I didn't think the Gulliver House garden had a monster tunnel. And I didn't think these were monsters.

Of course not. A four-year-old might be happy with that explanation. But I wasn't.

It was just, I no idea what else they were.

Mutants maybe? Animal testing gone horribly wrong? Released from a secret laboratory?

I just didn't know.

But maybe – just maybe – Oliver had actually seen something. And whatever that something was – a hole? a burrow? actually a tunnel? – maybe I could shoo the moth thing through it, and block it up.

Well, it was worth a try. Because I wanted the moth thing gone.

Fast.

Chapter Seven
The Bristling Thing

You can NOT rush a four year old.

First Oliver had to show me his wormery. Then he had to show me his stone collection. And then he had to show me his bunny. A fat black bunny lolloping around in a little run at the bottom of the garden.

'Big Bunny,' said Oliver proudly. 'Say hello to Finn.' Big Bunny stuck up a paw in greeting.

I gaped. How did he get her to do that? How?

'Big Bunny,' said Oliver, wagging a finger. 'Play dead.'

Big Bunny lay down. Completely still.

After that, Oliver was ready, so we set off for the fence.

'I'm currently too short to climb the fence,' Oliver informed me, as he wriggled underneath.

Through the fence and on the path, Oliver stuck his hand – small and sticky, but with a firm grip – in mine. 'Let's skip, Finn,' he said.

So off we went – skip skip skip – along the path through the woods, towards Gulliver House.

'I like your monsters,' Oliver said, pointing his feet carefully as he skipped. 'They're funny. One monster, the remarkably fluffy one with the big horn and the black tongue, let me stroke it.'

Skipping and gaping is not easy to do at the same time – but I managed it.

'It had a caterpillar, a most astonishingly big one, caught in its mane,' Oliver said, grabbing hold of my other hand too, and skipping sideways. 'So I took the caterpillar out and it crawled away. Heaven knows where it went.'

A caterpillar, astonishingly big… Well, I knew exactly where it went. My wardrobe.

Suddenly – extremely suddenly – Oliver stopped skipping. 'This is the tree I have to stop at, Finn,' he said. 'Mummy says.'

And he pointed straight ahead towards a big huddle of trees just inside the Gulliver House garden.

'And there is the monster tunnel,' he said. 'But sometimes it's not.'

What? What did he mean?

Well, there was no time to find out, because just then something – mainly bristles and teeth – went scuttling through the trees behind us. Then I heard a skidding sound, and a yelp, and high-pitched bawling noises. Lots of them…

It was behind a tree, flat on its back, mouth wide open, wailing its head off.

The bristling thing. The thing I saw scuttling across the garden last night.

Close up, it looked very young. The size and shape of a football, with piggy nostrils, a bawling mouth, long eyelashes, four paws, a stumpy tail – and everything else was bristles.

It also had jaggedy teeth in its mouth, which clattered furiously together when it saw me and Oliver. Before I could stop him, Oliver crouched down, and gave it a stroke.

The thing tried to bite his hand off.

Oliver looked astonished, then stern. 'No, no, no,' he said, wagging his finger.

The thing tried to bite his finger off.

I grabbed Oliver's hand before it managed to. 'No!' I said.

'No?' said Oliver, staring at me like I'd said something baffling. 'Why not?'

Why not? Was he blind? 'Look at its teeth,' I said.

Oliver looked. 'They're very pointy and sharp,' he observed. Then he looked at me with his saucer eyes. 'But monsters never bite children. Or hurt children. Or eat children. Mummy says.'

Oh.

'And,' said Oliver, 'I asked Mummy if I was allowed to stroke the monsters, and Mummy said yes. Mummy says all the monsters in your garden are lovely monsters, and I can play with them as much as I like.'

Oh, now this was tricky – but I had to say something. Because sending Oliver home with missing fingers and having him tell his mum a monster bit them off was quite likely to get me in trouble.

'Oliver,' I said. 'Most monsters in the garden are lovely monsters. But some monsters are bad. So you must never EVER pat a monster, or try to be friends with a monster, in case it's a bad one.'

'Never, Finn?' said Oliver, eyes popping.

'Only if you're with me,' I said. 'And I say you can.' Because, who knew? Maybe some of them *were* lovely... Maybe.

'So Mummy was lying?' said Oliver and – oh, no – his bottom lip was trembling.

I felt my brain beginning to ache. How to handle this?

'Mummy didn't mean to lie,' I said. 'She just doesn't know about the bad monsters in the garden. No one does. Just us.'

And that's when it hit me. I had proof. Right here.

I could pick the bristling thing up. Take it to Mum, show the PPs. Then they'd have to believe me. About this – and about the moth thing…

Except it wasn't that easy.

The bristling thing had a thorn in its paw, which explained the yelp. A big spiky thorn, which had to come out. Because a bristling thing in extreme pain was a lot more likely to use its teeth on me if I tried to carry it.

So I stroked its bristles – carefully, well away from its teeth. I had a quiet chat with it, explained what I was about to do. Then I tickled it under the chin – at least, where I reckoned a chin might be – and it started purring, and batted its eyelashes at me – and it really did have quite lovely eyes.

Well… compared to the rest of it.

I judged it was ready. Calmed down. It seemed

to understand I meant it no harm, that I was here to help.

So I moved my hand towards the thorn, and small nervous smoke rings started coming out of the bristling thing's nostrils – which should have warned me, but didn't.

I gave the thorn one quick yank and pulled it out. The bristling thing leapt up. It gave a yelp of pain. A blast of flames and sparks shot out of its nostrils, and set fire to the sleeve of my hoodie.

I wriggled out of my burning top fast as I could, then I chucked the hoodie to the ground, and got busy stamping out all the flames.

And while I was doing all that, the bristling thing scuttled off.

Then I heard a noise – BOOM! – along with a sudden flash of light.

I looked up and saw Oliver clapping his hands and pointing. 'The monster tunnel!' he beamed. 'It was there.'

But it wasn't. Not when I looked.

Nothing was.

And the bristling thing was gone.

Chapter Eight
Big Trouble

I took Oliver home, then slunk around the garden for a bit, because I knew Mum would yell at me about my hoodie when I went in.

But she didn't.

Because when I went in Mum yelled at me about something else.

'Finn!' she shouted, as soon as I stuck my head round the kitchen door. 'How could you? Frightening a small child like that. Telling Oliver there were bad monsters in the garden. I'm ashamed of you.'

Oh no.

Clearly Oliver had been talking – too much. Told his mum all about the bad monsters, and so she had told my mum…

So Mum carried on yelling at me. A lot.

And when I tried to tell Mum what had really happened, how we had a mutant fire-breather in our garden, Mum just blocked her ears and started screeching, 'GO! TO! YOUR! ROOM!'

And all the time, the PPs sat at the kitchen table, listening in, goggle-eyed.

A bit later, they came clattering in to my bedroom.

Mo was chortling. 'Lily has an extremely stupid idea,' she said, then screeched with laughter. 'Tell him your idea, Lily. Tell him it!'

Lily stared down at the bows on her shoes, looking bothered and confused. 'I think you might be telling the truth,' she mumbled. 'Because you're the sort of idiot who finds ambushes and traps and cutting holes in sisters' pyjamas funny. But I don't think you would be that mean to a four-year-old. You just wouldn't. However fed up you are.'

You know what? There are times – not often – when I feel like giving Lily a great big smacking kiss, and this was one of them.

Not that I did.

'So...' screeched Mo, handing me her camera, which she'd won – Mo's hobby also being entering competitions. 'Get some proof of these… mutants. By dinnertime.'

★ ★ ★

It took me two hours to find the moth thing.

It was lurking, deep in the woods. Crouched low, head down, teeth crunching. Eating a small heap of grey fur and guts and squishy bits – I had no idea what.

I felt something icy cold creep through my insides.

Because as it ate, as it crunched each mouthful in its sharp little teeth, the moth thing grew. Right in front of my eyes.

An inch. Maybe two. Maybe more.

And it was already bigger than a cat. Quite a bit bigger.

It's hard holding a camera steady when your hands are shaking and your knees are knocking – but I did my best.

I pressed the button.

Click. I took the picture. Then I checked to see how it came out. Perfect.

I crept closer. Took another picture, just to be sure – and that was when the moth thing spun round.

It hissed. It reared up. It flapped its horrible sprawling wings at me. It waggled its bony insect legs – arms, whatever they were. It took one jerking threatening step towards me.

I knew what it was saying. *Go away. Leave me to my dinner…*

So I did.

Fast.

I dodged up through the trees, back on to the path, towards the Gulliver House garden. But as I ran to the gate I turned around, just to see if the moth thing was behind me, flapping and hissing through the trees…

Big mistake.

Because turning round to check behind me, meant I didn't notice what was in front of me: A great big tree root. Stuck right across the path.

So I went hurtling over it, head-first, into a rolling tumble, and the camera – Mo's precious camera – went flying out of my hand.

It flew out of the woods. High across the garden in a great big arc. And smashed straight into a tree trunk at high speed.

It was destroyed.

★ ★ ★

Mo raided my piggy bank. She took every single coin and note in it. 'Idiot!' she screeched, right in my face. Then she flashed her Twin Club badge at me, stuck her nose in the air, and walked off.

Lily wouldn't even look at me – which was worse.

I waited until Mo was out of the way. Downstairs, bashing out notes on the big piano and wailing some horrible tune over the top of it.

Then I pushed Lily's door open. Because I wanted to see her alone.

Lily glared. She clearly didn't want to see me. So I held out the book in my hand.

Fibbing Fergus.

One last try to convince Lily about the moth thing.

Fibbing Fergus is the book me and Lily have used to swear we're telling the truth, since we were five years old.

It's the story of a boy – Fergus – who steals a book of goblins from a witchy neighbour, but says he didn't. Then, after that, every time Fergus fibs a goblin shoots out of the book and plays a crafty trick on him.

Mo said *Fibbing Fergus* was boring, and that she only liked books about girls. But me and Lily loved it. We made Mum read it to us every night for three weeks after I got it.

And then Lily lost her gel pens and made me stick my hand on *Fibbing Fergus* and swear I hadn't stolen them. She said a goblin would get me if I was lying. Which we both sort of believed, being five.

So I did swear on *Fibbing Fergus* – and that night she found her gel pens, stuck down the side of her bed.

Me and Lily used *Fibbing Fergus* a lot after that. We stopped believing in the goblin, of course. But we never EVER told a lie, not with a hand on *Fibbing Fergus*.

It was sort of a sacred thing. A shared thing. Just me and Lily.

And now… well, it was time for *Fibbing Fergus* again.

So I stuck one hand on *Fibbing Fergus* and looked straight at Lily. 'I swear the moth thing is real,' I said.

Then I waited. I really, really hoped it would work.

It didn't.

Looks started flitting across Lily's face. Unhappy, upset, betrayed sort of looks. The sort of looks that said a sacred childhood memory had just been destroyed by a brother.

Followed by another look.

Fury.

'You will seriously regret that,' Lily hissed, eyes glittering and hard. Then she pushed me out of her bedroom and slammed the door shut.

As for Mum, Mo went screeching to her about the camera, so Mum shoved a whole lot of buckets and mops and cleaning stuff at me and marched me out to the sheds.

'Clear them up,' she yelled, right in my face, glaring so hard her eyebrows actually met right in the middle.

The sheds were a mess. All afternoon I scrubbed. I mopped. I tidied. I sorted...

And all the while my brain did somersaults and twizzles and twirls trying to make sense of it all. But I couldn't. None of it.

And every rustle, every flutter, got me twitching. I kept thinking I saw two bulging eyes peering in at me. A flash of sludgy green wings. Something waggling. Something strutting. Something hissing...

But I didn't. Not until later.

★ ★ ★

It was dark, and I was up in my bedroom by the window, when I saw it again.

A shadow. Flapping across the garden, silhouetted against the moon – with a black bundle clutched between its front legs. A bundle with two floppy ears...

And next morning Big Bunny was missing.

Chapter Nine
Big Bunny is Back

'Mummy says Big Bunny has gone to heaven,' said Oliver. He gave a sniff. He looked up at me with big sad eyes. 'Is Mummy wrong again, Finn?'

'No, Mummy's right this time,' I said.

Oliver looked sadly at Big Bunny's empty hutch. The splintered door. The mangled and shredded remains. The scratch marks and tooth marks, where something had ripped and clawed and chewed its way in.

Poor Big Bunny. Picked up, dragged off in those bony legs. What a horrible fate.

Oliver sniffed again.

I crouched down, and gave his nose a wipe. Well – someone had to, and Oliver didn't look like he was planning to.

'Big Bunny will be happy in heaven,' I said. 'Because God grows carrots.'

'And lettuces?' said Oliver, a small fat tear rolling slowly out of each eye.

'All vegetables,' I said.

'Did a monster eat Big Bunny?' said Oliver.

'I don't know,' I said – but I did know. I knew exactly what had eaten Big Bunny. A mutant moth thing that grew so fast I could see it happening.

Then I heard snuffling and padding paws. And a face appeared through the fence.

A twitching, snuffling face.

A face with a pink nose and long whiskers.

A face with black floppy ears…

Big Bunny.

What?

No. That could NOT be Big Bunny. It just couldn't. The moth thing got her. I saw it with my own eyes.

But while I was standing, gaping and baffled, Oliver was already wriggling under the fence.

'Big Bunny,' he shouted, beaming, and running as fast as he could towards her. 'You're back!'

But Big Bunny shot off down the path – the left-hand path. The one that went deeper and deeper into the woods.

'Big Bunny,' Oliver wailed. 'Come back!' Then he shot off too, fast as his sturdy little legs could take him. Following Big Bunny…

A feeling went creeping and crawling right up my spine. A feeling that something was very wrong. And I knew. I just knew.

That was NOT Big Bunny.

So I leapt the fence. Hurled myself down the path and grabbed Oliver's arm – just as he skidded towards Big Bunny…

Or whatever it was.

Because something was happening to Big Bunny. Her floppy ears were getting longer, thinner, wagglier… Her face was getting flatter, wider… Her black fur was turning green – sludgy green with stripes. She was sprouting wings… And long insecty legs… And growing…

I ran. Grabbed hold of Oliver's arm, and ran. I sprinted back up the path like I was running for Olympic gold, half pulling, half-dragging him along. I bundled him over the fence, and threw myself after him.

And behind us, I heard flapping wings wheeling through the trees. I heard shrieking noises – horrible shrieking noises, worse than Mo makes – gradually fading away.

Then it was gone.

And Oliver was jumping up and down, gnashing his teeth. 'BAD monster!' he yelled, shaking his fist at the woods. 'You pretended to be Big Bunny. My bunny! You did BAD magic! You tried to trick me!'

Then a whistle blew out. Three sharp shrills, coming from the top of Oliver's garden...

Because baby Arthur was starting to hatch.

★ ★ ★

So that was it. Oliver went off to his granny's — and I went indoors. Quaking, and thinking.

It was time for action. Time for a plan...

A trap. My biggest and best trap EVER. A huge pit — bigger than me — big enough for a moth thing. Disguised with a false floor to make it look as if it was solid ground.

I'd bait it with Wolfgang, tuck a lump of steak from the fridge underneath him. I'd wait. Crouch in the shadows, waiting for the moth thing to see Wolfgang, smell the meat, swoop down, land — and go plummeting straight into my pit.

Then I'd hurl stuff at it. Stuff from the shed. Netting. Mesh. Bits of fencing. Mouse traps. Wooden posts. Giant flowerpots. Keep it busy trying to bite and claw and struggle its way out.

Busy for long enough to get Mum. Show her. Get her to call someone – the police, the council, pest control. Whoever was in charge of dealing with moth things.

That would work as a plan, I thought, ignoring some small niggling feelings I was having. Yes. It would.

And I was starting my plan right now.

Except Mum also had a plan for the rest of that day.

I knew it wasn't worth me saying I had my own plan. Not when my plan was building a trap for a moth thing...

So I didn't. And by the time Mum's plan – mainly shopping for school stuff and trudging round a town – were done, it was dark.

Never mind, I thought. One day won't make much difference. Because how tall can a moth thing get? Three foot? Four foot, tops?

Yes. About that, I thought.

Because even if the moth thing was still growing – and it probably wasn't – it could NOT grow more than that. It just couldn't.

That's what I actually thought.

Silly, silly me.

Chapter Ten
The Trap

I got digging early the next day. I chose a spot
inside the woods – but only just. I wanted to be
close to the garden. Close enough to run for it if
I needed to…

The PPs came and watched me dig, Twin Club
badges sparkling.

'That's not a den,' Mo said, curling her lip and
forgetting they weren't talking to me. 'We know
it's not.'

I'd told Mum I was building a den for the PPs.
To say sorry for being an idiot.

'We know it's a trap,' Mo said. 'And we know
it's for us. We know you think we'll fall into it. We
SO won't.'

I felt miserable. Alone.

'If you've got nothing better to do than stand

there yakking on at me,' I snapped, 'just go away.'

'Oh, we've got better things to do,' said Mo, cackling and sticking her nose in the air. 'We totally have.'

Lily didn't say anything. Just glared at me with a vicious sort of gleam in her eye.

So I dug and I dug and I dug. I dug all morning.

But something happened as I dug. The niggling feelings I ignored yesterday came back. Then the niggling feelings turned themselves into questions.

I tried to ignore the questions, but I knew they were there. Questions like …

– Is a stuffed dog with a lump of steak underneath actually going to convince a moth thing it's dinner?

– Suppose the moth thing just swoops on the stuffed dog and doesn't even try to land?

– Is a moth thing that can crunch up the door of a rabbit hutch going to be stopped by some stuff from the shed long enough for me to get Mum?

By lunchtime I was fed up with digging and fed up with questions.

But I carried on, all afternoon. I dug until my arms were aching. I dug until my fingers were in blisters. And every time I felt like stopping,

I thought about that fat furry face. Those slitty nostrils. Those bulging eyes. And I carried on.

But still the questions niggled away. More and more of them. Worse questions than the morning ones. Questions like…

– If a smallish moth thing grows a few inches as it eats, does a bigger moth thing grow a lot more inches as it eats?

– How fast would a moth thing have to grow to be too big for a boy-sized pit?

– If a moth thing is thinking of eating a four-year-old for dinner on a Tuesday, what is it thinking of eating for dinner on a Wednesday?

And most of all…

– Is this trap a brilliant plan, or the kind of plan a boy comes up with when he can't think of any other plan whatsoever?

And the more I dug, the more questions niggled.

By the time the sky was growing dark, and the last shadows were stretching across the garden, my pit was so big I had to prop a ladder up to get out.

That had to be a big enough pit to trap a moth thing.

Had to be.

So, as the sun sank behind the trees, I put Wolfgang and his steak in position, I forked the last leaves across the false floor. I was ready to go back down the garden, crouch in the shadows, and wait for the moth thing.

But I didn't need to wait.

Because, just then, I heard it. The *flap flap flap* of giant wings.

And then I saw its shadow, way down the garden, by the woods. Its great big shadow.

And at that moment, I knew what I'd feared all along.

My plan. My trap. The pit. The netting. The mesh. All of it was useless.

The moth thing was too big. Much, MUCH too big.

And then I did start panicking. A lot.

Chapter Eleven
Cornered

I shot off like I had rocket fuel for blood. Sheer total terror powered my legs across the garden, towards the house, towards the nearest door…

The front door.

I charged up the big stone steps. I grabbed the front door handle, and wrenched it round.

'Please let it be unlocked, please,' I heard myself babbling.

It was.

So I hurled myself through, slammed it shut behind me, and bolted it.

Safe. For now.

'Mum!' I yelled, charging through the hallway. 'Mum! Where are you?'

I flung doors open. Checked room after room after room.

But Mum wasn't there. Not anywhere.

I slumped in the kitchen. Where was she? Where was she?

Then – *clack clack clack* – I heard two pairs of feet in the corridor.

Lily and Mo.

They came prancing into the kitchen, flashing their Twin Club badges, grinning and giggling at me.

Then they stopped – both of them. They stood stock still and stared straight out through the window behind me.

Their mouths dropped open. Their eyes stretched wide, and they started to shudder.

I turned around.

It was there. Outside the window. A monstrous great head. Staring in at us.

It moved past the window, jerking its head, like dinosaurs do. I could hear its feet. *Thud... thud... thud.*

I ran and slammed the bolts across the back door.

It moved on to the side window.

Thud... thud... thud.

It turned and looked straight in. And moved on again.

Mo clutched on to my arm. 'It's looking for a way in,' she said, whimpering. 'It's going round the house. It'll find a way in. It absolutely will.'

'It can't,' I said. 'The doors are bolted. The windows are too small. It absolutely can't.'

Lily clutched at my other arm. 'Mum,' she said. 'She went up the garden. To the compost. Where is she? Where is she?'

I didn't answer. Didn't know what to say.

Something must have happened to Mum. Somewhere out there. Something –

No. I wasn't thinking about that.

Thud… thud… thud.

'I'm scared,' said Mo, in a teeny quavering voice that didn't sound like her at all. 'Really scared.'

'Me too,' said Lily.

'And me,' I said.

Then we all huddled together in the middle of the kitchen. All quavering, quaking, panicking.

'We'll ring,' I said, scratching around for a plan. 'Say the house is on fire. They'll send someone. Big engines. Grown-ups. And it can't get in. As long as we stay in the house, we're safe.'

That was when I realized something. The thudding had stopped. There was no noise at all.

Except one.

A small noise. The noise of something slithering…

'What is it?' said Lily, clutching on to me. 'What's that noise?'

I knew what it was.

It was the noise of something big that had shapeshifted into something small, something small and slithering – a small slithering thing that could flatten itself enough to get in anywhere.

Anywhere.

Even from outside a house… to inside a house.

It came right into the hallway. Then the slithering noise stopped.

And I knew why. I knew that out there, in the hallway, the thing was changing shape again. Changing and growing and growing and growing…

Back into something bigger.

Something much MUCH bigger.

And then we heard it again. Inside. Closer.

Thud… thud… thud.

I looked at Mo and Lily. 'It's in the hallway,' I whispered.

'But… how? How can it be?' screeched Mo, really panicking. 'Its wings will get stuck in the railings! Its head will get squished in the doorways! It's too big to come along the corridors… Isn't it? ISN'T IT?'

Lily was looking at me, eyes full of terror. 'You said we were safe inside,' she said. 'You said it couldn't get in.'

'I was wrong,' I said. 'We're not safe. Not in here. Not anywhere.'

I don't know what I thought the PPs would do. Faint flat out on the floor? Swoon into a kitchen chair? Throw their arms in the air and run around screaming?

They didn't do any of that.

They looked at each other – and they both got this ferocious light in their eyes.

Mo rolled up her sleeves. 'We have to fight it,' she said. 'Totally.'

Lily was nodding. 'We have the advantage,' she said. 'There's one of it, and three of us.'

'We'll drive it down the garden,' Mo said.

'Into Finn's trap,' said Lily. 'Then we'll – I don't know – sit on it, until help comes.'

They each grabbed one of Mum's big shopping bags and started filling them. They scooped up tins and bottles from the cupboards. Apples and pears from the fruit bowl. Plates and mugs and bowls. Mo even flung the fridge open and started grabbing stuff.

I could NOT believe it. What did my sisters think they were they doing?

This thing – this monstrous moth thing – must be ten feet tall. At least. With wings and teeth and claws. And my sisters were planning to drive it down the garden with some tins, a bit of crockery and fruit, and a squirt of whipped cream from the fridge.

They had no chance whatsoever.

But as I looked at them, scooping up ammunition, gritting their teeth to stop them chattering, trying to look tough and hard and mean – as if that would bother a moth thing – to my utter astonishment, I felt a glow of pride.

My sisters might be idiots. But they were heroic idiots.

And also so busy with their ridiculous plan that they didn't notice me pocketing the key to the kitchen door.

'Ready?' said Lily. 'When I count to three, we'll open the door and charge.'

'Ready,' Mo said.

Then they both looked at me.

'Ready,' I said.

We all punched a fist in the air.

'One,' said Lily – but I didn't wait for two, or three.

I just ran out of the kitchen door, slammed it shut and locked it. Then I ran along the corridor towards the hallway.

Because if the monster was going to eat someone, it might as well be me.

Chapter Twelve
The Plan

There it was. A huge hissing shape. Towering up in the big square hallway of Gulliver House.

I took one look at it – its vast sprawling wings, its wide open mouth full of teeth, rows and rows of them, jagged as saws...

And I changed my mind.

That thing, that vicious waggling monster, was NOT having me for dinner. Not me, not anyone.

Not if I could help it.

I ran for the front door. Threw back the bolts. Kicked the huge doors wide open.

'Come and get me, you great ugly monster!' I yelled.

It lunged at me on its huge insect legs. I threw myself sideways, rolled across the hallway, and ran for the stairs.

I knew I had one advantage, and only one. I was small and nimble. And the moth monster most definitely wasn't.

I ducked and dodged up the stairs as two jets of green foam blasted right past my ears.

I hurtled, panicking, along the landing, thinking: what now? Where can I go? What can I do?

The moth monster stared straight up at me, eyes gleaming. Then it hissed, and started to flap its great sprawling wings.

I could hardly breathe. Hardly think.

It was going to come flapping and swooping up through the hallway. Up to the landing, pick me up in its horrible monster legs, and then… THEN…

Then a plan burst into my head. An impossible, ridiculous, stupendously brilliant plan. A plan for someone small and nimble…

So I clambered over the railings.

And jumped.

It was the biggest, most terrifying leap of my life.

A giant leap straight down. Straight for the one place those huge jagged teeth couldn't get at me.

The back of the moth monster's head.

I grabbed hold of its antlers – thick greasy tubes, rough as sandpaper. I locked my arms round the hideous waggling things. I wedged my feet where its great sprawling wings met its fat furry body, and I clung on.

I was going to RIDE that horrible hissing thing. Ride it out of the front door – and away from Gulliver House. Ride it to town. To a place with lights. With people.

Because even grown-ups would notice a ten-foot moth monster pounding by. Flattening bus stops. Crushing parked cars. With a boy clinging on to its antlers, his feet wedged above its wings.

The grown-ups would HAVE to believe in monsters then.

They could call in the troops. Get helicopters tracking us from the air. Parachute special forces in with stun guns. Get diggers building giant monster traps. Get rid of it – somehow.

Yes. Grown-ups would sort out the moth thing – they just had to see it first. And I was going to make sure they did.

Only – of course – it wasn't that simple.

The moth monster took one giant leap out of the huge front doors, another giant leap down the big stone steps of Gulliver House – and I realized the power of the thing.

I couldn't steer it. I couldn't control it. All I could do was keep clinging on.

It shrieked and hissed and thrashed with rage. It kept twisting its huge head, trying to bite me, trying to shake me off.

It crashed its huge bony wings against my back as it flapped and flapped and tried to take off – but it couldn't, not with my entire weight wedged just above its wings.

So I clung on, as the moth monster took great bucking strides... but not towards town, like I planned.

Oh no.

It was heading down the Gulliver House garden and straight for the woods.

It leapt the gate in one big bound – and landed straight on the garden fork.

The prongs must have hit a sensitive spot, because it yowled, and stopped dead.

I wasn't expecting that.

Which was why I lost my grip on its antlers. And why I went hurtling straight over its head. And hurtling down...

Into my trap.

★ ★ ★

I'll never forget it. Even when I'm sitting in a rocking chair with grey hair and no teeth, I'll never forget it.

The huge furry head looking over the side of my trap, eyes bulging like shiny black cannonballs…

The bony legs reaching in and lifting me out as if I weighed no more than a bag of sugar…

The tin of baked beans that came shooting out of nowhere and clanged off the moth monster's head…

And Lily and Mo, pounding through the shadows in the garden, armed with their shopping bags.

'Get off my brother!' Mo yelled at the moth monster, leaping the garden gate. Then she charged right up to it and squirted in both eyes with the whipped cream.

Lily was cracking plates over its head. The moth monster ducked and dodged and hissed and shrieked.

But it wasn't enough. I knew it wasn't.

The shopping bags would soon be empty. And what then?

Only a miracle could help us now.

And we got one.

BOOM!

There was a flash of light, and the bristling thing came scuttling down the garden and under the gate. Clattering its teeth, nipping at the moth monster's legs and shooting out tiny little angry flames.

But that wasn't the miracle. Oh no. Because…

BOOM!

There was a another flash of light, and another bristling thing appeared. But this was a much bigger bristling thing. Much, MUCH bigger. Big as a building, looming out of the garden.

The big bristling miracle flattened the gate completely under one gigantic paw. A sheet of flames came blasting out of its enormous piggy nostrils. There was a burning singeing smell, as the moth monster started scrabbling to put out the flames on its antlers.

It cowered as the gigantic miracle lumbered towards it.

All of a sudden, the moth monster – which looked so big a few moments ago – looked tiny. Tiny and totally terrified.

It started flapping its wings, fast as it could. Then it took off, and swooped over the squashed

gate and the bristling miracle thing. It swerved across the garden, straight towards the huddle of trees. And…

BOOM!

There was a flash of light, dazzling as lightning. A glimpse of a vast sizzling circle hovering in the air.

And the moth monster was gone.

Chapter Thirteen
The Gorgle

The moth monster must have got Mum with its squirters. We found her standing next to the compost heap, still as a statue, arm outstretched, holding a bucket of vegetable peelings, and dripping green foam.

It took three hours before Mum gave a blink and opened her eyes. And it took a lot more hours before she gave up trying to work out what had happened to her.

But we didn't tell. No point.

Besides, Mum would never EVER live in Gulliver House if she knew there was some kind of monster tunnel in the garden.

And, well…

Seeing the spring sunlight in the garden, all the little flowers poking up… Hearing Oliver galloping about in his paddock doing monster impressions for baby Arthur in his pram… Knowing a bristling thing the size of a large dinosaur is now my friend, and may pop back through the tunnel to say hello…

Well, with all that, I didn't want to leave Gulliver House.

Not any more.

As for the PPs… did they thank me for quite possibly saving their lives?

No. They sat on me.

The day after it was all over, they came barging into the fifth room – where I was busy practising my lassooing skills on Wolfgang – clutching their Twin Club badges.

I thought they were about to sob with gratitude. Tell me how lucky they were to have the bravest brother in the world. Vow to burn their Twin Club badges on the bonfire Mum had just got going up near the enormous patch of mud she calls the vegetable garden.

I was wrong.

The pair of them flattened me. They forced me down on to the rug, and both sat on me.

'Do the hero thing EVER again…' Lily said, curls bobbing, eyes glittering, and brandishing her Twin Club badge. 'And these go back on. Forever.'

'We so totally do NOT appreciate being locked in a kitchen while you have all the fun,' screeched Mo, blue eyes glaring, bracelets jangling, and fingernails pinching a really soft bit of my arm. 'And I had a perfectly good plan. Which – by the way – if you had also filled a shopping bag instead of deciding you were going to hog the whole monster fight to yourself, MIGHT have worked.'

Then they both started pummelling me, so I squished deeper into the rug...

And I felt two shapes, like hinges, digging into my back.

That's how we found it. A trapdoor under the rug. The way in to the secret room.

A panic room, that's what me and the PPs reckon it was. A room to hide in, in case of large or particularly vicious monsters. You flung open the trapdoor in the fifth room, hurtled down the steps, along a short corridor, up some more steps, through another trapdoor and into the secret room. The panic room. Safety.

It had supplies of tinned food, a toilet, everything you'd need. And something else...

A sketchbook. A big book full of drawings, belonging to Darwin Gulliver. Page after page of strange creatures. All with names. All with notes about them.

And on page 47, there it was. The moth monster. Shrieking and staring out of the page. With a name…

GORGLE

it said.

★ ★ ★

It's been three weeks now, and nothing horrible has come out of the monster tunnel.

Maybe something will. Maybe not. Who knows?

Because if the Gorgle is real – well, I expect all the others are too.

But I know one thing for sure.

Whatever comes through the monster tunnel, this time I won't be alone. Because me and the PPs – we're a team. And we'll be ready.

I hope.